AF522474

ULTIMATE INDIAN
CRICKET
CHAMPIONS

INDIA

INDIA

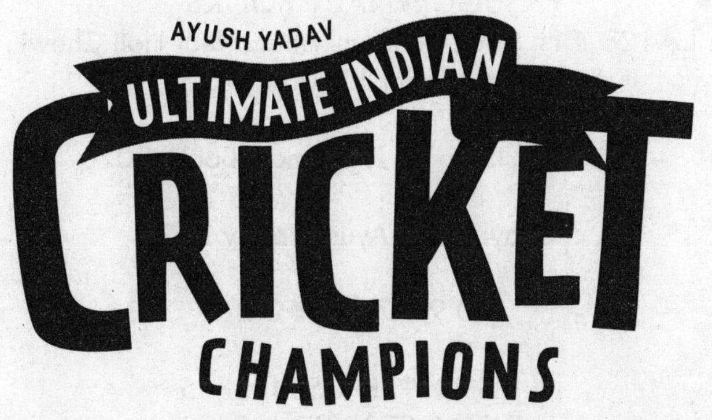

HARDIK PANDYA

juggernaut

JUGGERNAUT BOOKS
C-I-128, First Floor, Sangam Vihar, Near Holi Chowk,
New Delhi 110080, India

First published by Juggernaut Books 2026

10 9 8 7 6 5 4 3 2 1

P-ISBN: 9789353455255
E-ISBN: 9789353452490

Typeset in Futura Std by R. Ajith Kumar, Noida

Printed at Thomson Press India Private Limited

For my mom and dad,
whose love, sacrifices and unwavering
faith kept me moving.

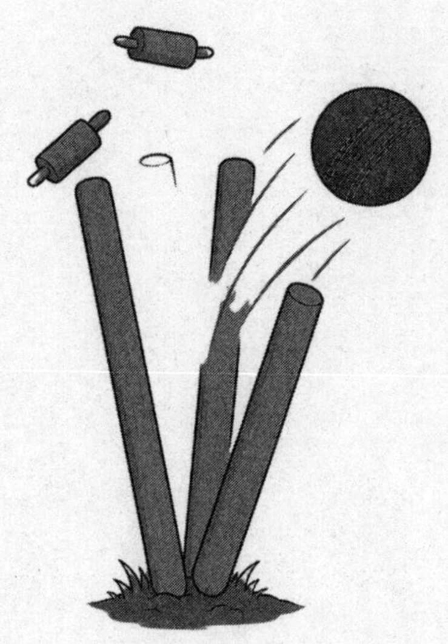

CONTENTS

1

BUILT FOR THE BIG STAGE

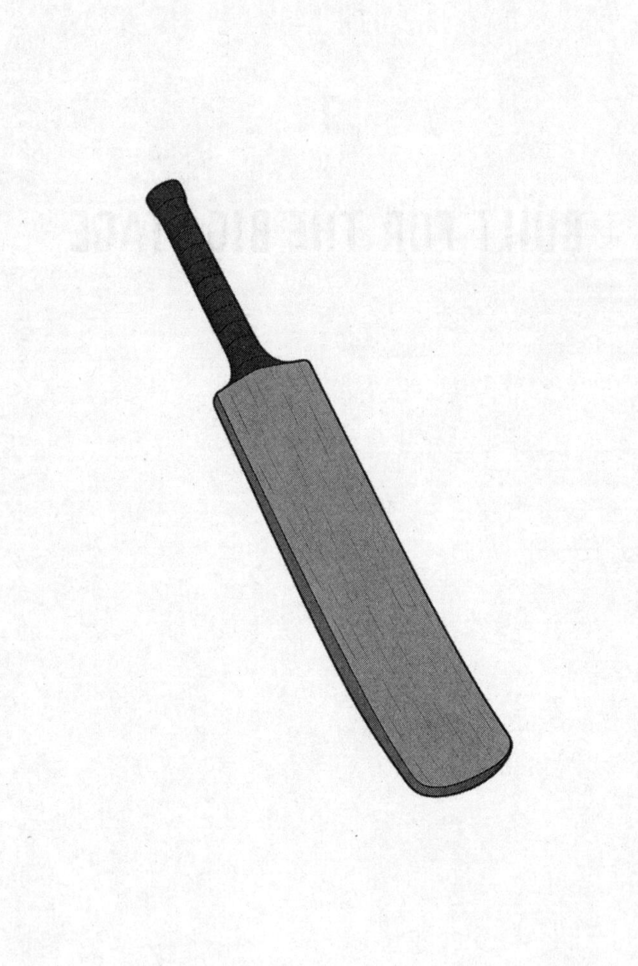

The night air in Barbados is thick and warm. The stadium is glowing under bright lights, and the crowd is loud – so loud that the sounds are jumping and dancing in the air. Blue jerseys fill the stands. Flags wave and hearts beat fast. It is the T20 World Cup final, and India is playing against South Africa.

India decides to bat – their innings being a roller coaster of early aggression, a rebuild in the middle overs and a late surge. The pitch was dry, and the pressure of finals was reason enough to set a target. As Captain Rohit Sharma and Virat Kohli jog up to the crease, bats in their hands and ready to play, thousands of fans cheer for them from the stands. Virat takes the strike and immediately finds his rhythm, hitting three boundaries in the first over and collecting 15 runs for the team. A thunderous roar erupts from the spectators dressed in blue, only to be silenced by Keshav Maharaj in the second over. Rohit attempts a sweep shot against Keshav's full delivery, which doesn't go through, and Heinrich Klaasen takes a relatively simple catch.

Rohit's early exit follows Rishabh Pant's dismissal in the same over. Soon after, Heinrich Klaasen takes Suryakumar Yadav's catch towards a deep fine leg on Kagiso Rabada's delivery, leaving India in a very dicey position: 34/3. Virat now knows his team needs him to stay on the crease. When Axar Patel comes to bat, he plays aggressively, hitting 47 runs off 31 balls, while Kohli focuses on holding one end. Axar and Virat rebuild the match in the middle overs. Despite this early setback, India scores 176 runs in 20 overs with three wickets

INDIA

in hand, the highest-ever total in a T20 World Cup final. As the final over ends, you can see a sense of relief on the faces of Indian fans all over the world, be it in the stands or those sitting in front of their TVs.

The second innings starts with South Africa's chase. Their fans are notably tense as the chase for the highest-ever total in a final begins. They were right as early blows to the team come in the second over when Jasprit Bumrah bowls out Reeza Hendricks with his legendary outswing – a delivery that many commentators describe as 'the ball of the tournament'. In the third over, Aiden Markram tries to play a forceful drive to Arshdeep Singh's delivery, only for the ball to get caught by Rishabh Pant behind the stumps.

Soon comes the nightmare. Heinrich Klaasen, who is in 'beast mode', continuously hits the ball hard, sending it flying across the boundary repeatedly. The match feels like it is running away. South Africa is close. Very close. The

INDIA

scoreboard says they need only 26 runs from 24 balls. Every shot feels like a small punch to India's hopes.

It's the seventeenth over, and Hardik is called to bowl again. In the ninth over, he had already bowled out Tristan Stubbs, helping India keep the pressure on.

Hardik stands on the field, hands on the ball, eyes fixed ahead. He takes only a second to think about the first innings. India had fought well. Virat had played a beautiful knock, calm and strong, helping India reach 176 runs. It felt like a good score then. But now, under these lights, with Klaasen swinging his bat like thunder, the situation feels fragile.

India needs something special – a moment or maybe a miracle.

Hardik rubs the ball in his hands as he walks to his mark. He glances towards Rohit Sharma. No long talk. No big signals. Just a look. Years of playing together mean they don't need many words to communicate.

HARDIK
33

Hardik starts his run-up, and he knows it's time for him to play some cricket.

'It was a dream which actually came true. You know, from my shoulder, a big weight was kind of off. I think it was just a relief of six, seven, eight months, which I had [gone through] prior to that. I was really proud. The way I was able to stand, you know, and maybe not show a lot of emotions or how I have been going through. It just came off, the pressure of shoulder carrying such weights just came off, and I was like, yeah, finally I did it for the country.'

— HARDIK PANDYA

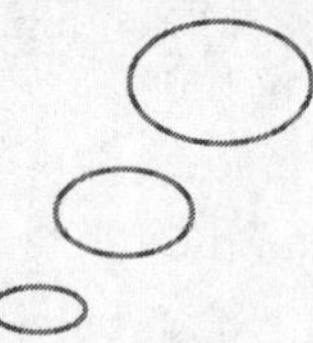

2

WHEN CRICKET TOOK OVER

PLUS
2000

Hardik comes home dusty, hungry and late once again. His school bag hangs loosely from one shoulder, a cricket ball bulging in one pocket, the corners of a battered notebook peeping out the other. He knows the questions that are coming. He always knows.

'How was school?' his father asks, not looking up at first.

Hardik hesitates to speak. School was fine, but cricket was better. The truth, as always, is somewhere in between.

His father looks at him, eyebrows raised – not angry, not disappointed, just tired. The tiredness that comes from long days and bigger dreams. 'Listen,' he says in a gentle tone.

Hardik pays attention to his father's words. 'Do you remember,' his father begins, 'why we came to Baroda?' Hardik looks down at his hands. He doesn't remember the day. He was only five then – too young to understand what it meant to leave home. But he remembers the story. He has heard it many times, albeit from different people: from his firm and proud father, Himanshu; his worried but hopeful mother, Nalini; and his elder brother, Krunal, who always adds, 'You were impossible even then.'

His father had once run a small car finance business in Surat. It was steady, safe, and sensible. But being sensible was not enough when the two boys wanted only one thing. Cricket – all day and almost every day. So, Himanshu Pandya shut down the business, packed up their lives and moved the family to Vadodara – then Baroda – chasing a dream that did not promise money or comfort, only uncertainty. Nalini came along quietly, carrying

her concerns like neatly folded clothes, but without a word of complaint.

They lived in a small, rented flat in Gorwa. Money was tight. Nalini used every rupee carefully. With limited resources, Maggi was the only sustenance Hardik and Krunal relied on. For nearly three years, both brothers survived on Maggi for both breakfast and lunch, earning them the nickname 'Maggi Brothers'. As yummy as it sounds, it wasn't enough, and they couldn't afford a proper athlete's meal. The car they travelled in to practice sessions and local matches was second-hand and tired, much like the man driving it. Their meals were simple, their worries were many, but cricket remained non-negotiable.

It was 1998, and as soon as the family had settled into their rented flat, Himanshu got both boys admitted to MK High School. Hardik was only five years old when his father approached Kiran More's International Cricket Academy to arrange proper training for the

MAGGI

boys. The academy at the time had a strict rule against admitting kids under twelve. It was only Himanshu's passion for his kids' future that convinced More to make an exception. And for the first time, the academy opened its doors for 'under-10' kids. As for school, Hardik carried his books with much less enthusiasm than he did his bat and ball. He studied until the ninth grade, long enough to realize that classrooms could not hold his interest the way a cricket field could. Eventually, he would stop going altogether – not because he lacked discipline, but because he had chosen his battle.

At the Kiran More Cricket Academy, he learned differently. Hardik didn't actually start as an enrolled student. He would hang around the boundaries and the back of the nets, while Krunal would be practising inside the nets. At times, Hardik would become the ball boy, running behind the nets, catching stray balls and throwing them back at the players. At other times, he would watch Krunal's sessions

attentively and then try to copy every move and shot from a distance. Eventually, he caught the eye of Kiran More. Keenly observing the new kid who constantly 'shadowed' the senior players, More saw a unique spark in Hardik's eyes. One day, he told Krunal to bring Hardik to the nets.

Hardik's and Himanshu's joys knew no bounds when Krunal broke the news to them. It was a moment of utmost happiness for a family who had left everything they had just so their children could receive proper cricket training. Amidst all the enjoyment, Himanshu and Nalini knew that there would be more pressure on them now. One more child officially joining the cricket academy meant double the fees for both the school and the academy. But that is something to be thought about later. Now is the time to be happy in the moment.

At this point, most of Hardik's days looked much like yours in school, except that they weren't. He went to school early, but his mind was always fixated on the evening sessions at

the academy. He would carry his cricket gear to school so he could go directly to the grounds as soon as the final bell rang. At the academy, it would be an intense physical training session of around six to eight hours, and by the time Hardik returned home, he was too exhausted for homework or exams. When Hardik failed his ninth-grade exams, instead of trying to balance things, he made the radical decision to drop out of school and focus entirely on the game. His father supported him, and from here began the journey of a boy who never looked back.

Once Hardik left school, his 'schooling' took place entirely at the academy. He would reach the academy at 7 a.m. every day, without fail. Nets became his classrooms. Sweat replaced ink. Mistakes were corrected not with red marks, but with longer spells, heavier balls and harder lessons. He batted with intent and bowled with pace. He played the game loudly enough to be noticed.

Selectors began to take notice. Not because his technique was perfect, but because his hunger was unmistakable. Hardik had no certificates or conventional qualifications to show. What he carried instead was an understanding of the game that could not be taught easily – an instinct for moments, a feel for pressure, a mind that evaluated situations faster than most. Cricket became his education, and it shaped him completely.

When he was eighteen, a Baroda-based coach, Sanath Kumar, watched him closely and uttered the words that changed the course of his journey: *switch to fast bowling*. Hardik followed the same.

Back home, cricket followed him everywhere. The narrow lanes became stadiums. Broken bricks marked the boundary. Old tennis balls whizzed past windows at dangerous angles. Hardik was a fiery player from the beginning. Even as a young kid, he didn't believe in

nudging the ball for singles. He would go all in. In Indian gully cricket, there's a common rule that if the ball goes into a house, you are out. Due to his aggressive technique, Hardik probably got out this way more than any other kid.

'Hardik!' someone would shout. 'Your turn to bat.'

Hardik never waited to be called twice. He played as if the match were a final. Argued like the rules were sacred. If someone tried to leave early, bat in hand, Hardik blocked the way. 'Finish the game first,' he would insist. 'You can't just leave.'

Windows broke, tempers flared and complaints arrived: 'Your son plays too roughly'; 'Your son shouts too much'; 'Your son takes the game too seriously.' Hardik was the one who usually argued to keep the game going. Later, even teams would drop him. The whispers spoke of 'attitude' issues. Hardik never understood that word. He wasn't arrogant. He was expressive

and emotional. He felt the game too deeply to stay silent about it.

Nalini often felt distressed, while Himanshu listened quietly and patiently.

One night, when Hardik rushed home after practice, his father sat beside him. Nalini stood at the door, listening. 'If you play,' Himanshu said, 'play properly. If you dream, dream fully.' Hardik nodded, already imagining floodlights where there were none.

Cricket was not a hobby in that house; it was hope. It was the reason his father worked harder every day. The reason Nalini remained troubled without expressing it. The reason is the two brothers pushed each other every day.

Hardik did not know where cricket would take him. But even then – walking on dusty streets, bat clutching too tight, eyes burning with belief – he knew one thing clearly. He was not playing for fun. He was playing for everything.

'My father was the only earning person at home. He suffered a heart attack – not one, but two and that too within one night. He almost got another attack six months later, but we were glad we reached the hospital in time. The financial problems started at the time ... we had no savings and perhaps we spent more than what we earned.'

— HARDIK PANDYA

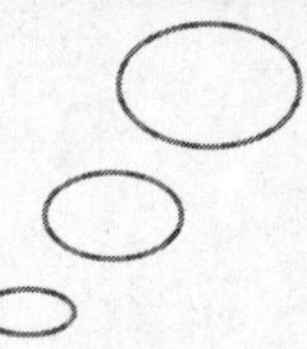

3

BEFORE THE LIGHTS, THERE WAS SILENCE

A hush falls over the stadium, like something is about to break. Sixteen years old, pads too big, dreams even bigger – Hardik tightens his shoelaces slowly, fingers pressing hard against the leather, as if control can be stitched into the moment.

Don't look at the scoreboard, he thinks. But he does. In bold letters, it shows **Baroda: 24/4. Mumbai: 306**. The stadium doesn't roar. It watches with bated breath. The walk to the crease feels longer than it is. Every step echoes, studs scraping cement. Bat tucked under his arm, helmet grille slicing the light, a boy walks in. A situation walks over him.

Stay. Just stay. Overs will pass. Bowlers will tire. Stay. He takes guard, looks around, and breathes deeply. He looks at the bowler and wonders if this is the moment that changes everything. Thoughts keep shifting with the blink of his eyes. One blink, one thought. Another blink, another thought. *Let me thrash the ball away right from the beginning.* Blink. *No, I should stay calm and be patient.* Blink. *What if my defensive game costs the team dearly?*

The first hour is a motley of sounds – seam, shouts, close fielders chattering, the ball thudding into gloves like gunshots. Hardik leaves deliveries, defends, gets hit, but doesn't flinch. Then time bends. Shot by shot, the panic leaves his shoulders. He waits, watches, studies, gauges the wicket, assessing the bounce, the seam, and the pace. Then, the shift. A poor delivery – short of length and crack. There goes the first boundary. The sound is different. It's cleaner and certain. *That's my ball* – a confidence seems to have taken over him.

As hours dissolve, sweat darkens his collar. His legs ache, and palms burn. Yet, he remains at the crease. It's been over eight hours. The sun moves across the sky like a slow clock, watching him grow up in real time. Hardik is no longer surviving; he is building.

Wickets keep falling at the other end – Shubham Agrawal, Kartik Kakade and others. But Hardik stays, building partnerships not on flair, but refusal. He strikes when he must. Blocks when he must. Punishes when he can: 228 runs and 391 balls. Twenty-nine fours and a six – each number is a brick pulling Baroda out of collapse. He doesn't just save the match, he drags it by the collar. Baroda take the first innings lead. A boy, batting at number four, turns a defeat into resistance.

'I was just playing my natural game ... I just waited for poor deliveries,' he says later. Simple words. But at the crease, it was war measured in patience.

Hardik is a right-handed batsman and a decent leg-spinner. He breaks partnerships when needed, a cricketer who wants to affect games, not decorate them. He had already played three Under-19 matches that year and scored 46 runs in his first U-19 match. Earlier that season, he had scored a 101 in his very first U-16 match against Gujarat. Nayan Mongia, watching Hardik's prowess, praised 'one of the best knocks I have seen'. A terrific all-rounder, a long way to go. But the road is not straight.

He has been dropped from the U-17 team in Baroda due to issues with the coach. And suddenly, cricket stops. Someone tells his brother he has an attitude problem. At home, a heavy silence sits at the dining table. A word floats in the air – 'attitude'. He is 16. He recalls the word from the neighbours' complaints during his gully cricket days. But *what does the word even mean?* He still can't figure it out. He laughs at the memory only later. But that moment weighs heavily.

At the same time, life tilts. His father, the sole bread earner, has a heart attack. It requires him to stop working. There's no regular income now. The small lifeline they had – about Rs 35,000 a year – from Hardik's U-16 or U-19 cricket is gone too. Everything stops at once. Hardik asks himself, *'Why us?'* The question circles his head like a bouncer he can't sway away from. Then grief hardens into a decision. *You want a fantastic life? Work. Just work.* That year, he became the highest run-scorer with 800 runs, yet the selectors did not pick him. He does 17 rounds of the ground, crying all the while as he runs – not for fitness, but for release. The following year, he is again, not picked. Doors stay shut. He shuts the world instead.

For the next three years, from ages 17 to 19, it's only cricket. No friends or a social life, no distractions. Just nets and sweat on repeat. Hardik shapes loneliness into discipline. He wants to prove himself, and he gets that opportunity.

His U-19 assistant coach and captain ask the selectors for one chance. Just one. Two selectors come to him with a clear message: he would get only one chance, and if he failed, nothing more could be done.

The boy who once walked in at 24 for 4 knows this feeling. Back against the wall. Clamour outside, voice inside. *Stay. Just stay.* And that is how Hardik Pandya begins – not in stadium lights, not in headlines, but in long days, empty pockets, sore legs, but a refusal to walk away.

Cricket, for him, was never just a game. It was the only door left open.

> *'Even difficult times, they don't last forever. It is important to be graceful, whether you win or lose.'*
>
> – HARDIK PANDYA

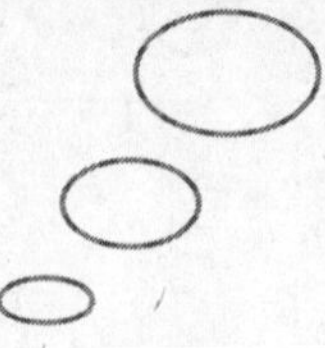

4

BELIEF BEATS THE ODDS

MUMBAI, JANUARY 2016

The Wankhede Stadium is alive. Not just loud – *alive*. Noise crashes down from every corner, bouncing off concrete, rolling across the grass. The air smells of sweat and hope and pressure. It's Friday night, and Baroda is chasing 163 against Uttar Pradesh in the Syed Mushtaq Ali T20 tournament in Mumbai.

In the dressing room, Hardik Pandya tightens his gloves. Now 22, he is all set to fly to Australia with the Indian team for the T20 league of the tour that follows the ODIs. But right now, none of that matters – not Australia, not the plane ride, not what happens tomorrow – only this.

Baroda loses Kedar Devdhar for 29 in the sixth over. The door opens. Hardik walks out at one down. His bat feels familiar in his hands. He remembers the last game – the one in his hometown. It was against Delhi when he had smashed 34 runs in a single over, and even though Baroda lost, the memory keeps him sharp and focused. Today will be different. He starts quietly. Then stronger. The ball begins to disappear – over the rope, into the crowd, again and again. By the end of the fifteenth over, the equation is clear: 63 runs needed from 30 balls.

Hardik looks around. The field, the bowlers, and the stands. He doesn't blink. The sixteenth over begins. Ravi Jangid, left-arm spinner, runs in. Hardik smashes three sixes in the first four balls. Cheers explode around him. At the other end, Irfan Pathan, the captain, is calm and watchful. He scored 26 out off 16 balls. Together, they turn the game on its head. In the nineteenth over, bowled by Ravi Thakur, the attack is ruthless. Two sixes, one four.

AVI

Hardik chooses his favourite place – mid-wicket. He's loved that region before, loved it during his stint in the last IPL with the Mumbai Indians and found himself loving it again here. The final blow is clean. A massive six that steals the victory. Hardik finishes unbeaten on 86 from 46 balls. Eight sixes, three fours.

Earlier, on 25, he was dropped at deep extra cover off Jangid. Cricket had smiled at him then. He had grabbed the moment with both hands. The partnership tells the real story: 83 runs in 37 balls with Irfan. They crushed Vidarbha's hopes, especially after the team had quickly taken wickets from Mrunal Devdhar, Deepak Hooda and Yusuf Pathan. That optimism didn't last.

With this powerful innings, Baroda won the match by six wickets in 19 overs. Hardik stands there, bat lowered, chest rising and falling. The crowd roars, but now it sounds distant. Muted, as if underwater.

Tonight, he is not just a young man heading to Australia. Tonight, he is a 'statement'. Hardik Pandya has arrived.

'When you get into the national side, the confidence level goes very high. I knew I'll get picked for the Australia series. I had to put in more hard work in the practice sessions and the helped me a lot. The kind of form I've had in the Syed Mushtaq Ali Twenty20 tournament, I am going (hoping) to carry it in Australia.'

— HARDIK PANDYA

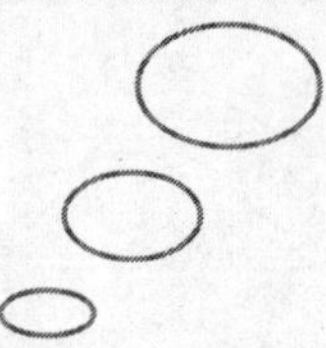

5

FEARLESS IN BLUE

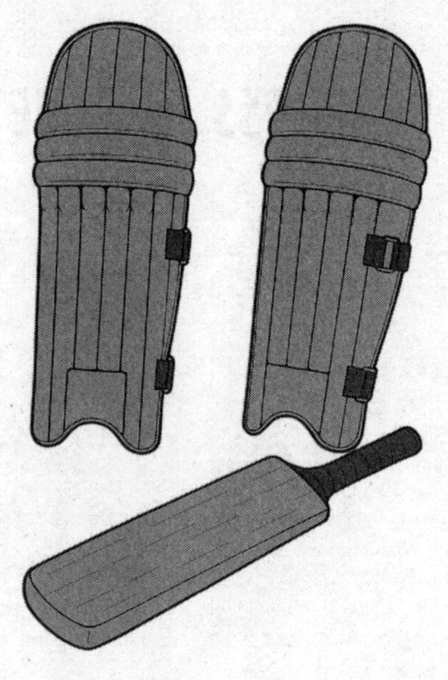

24 SEPTEMBER 2017, HOLKAR STADIUM, INDORE, MADHYA PRADESH

The buzz at Holkar Stadium never really settles. It swells, dips, swells again – drums, whistles, the low hum of mounting expectations. Floodlights bleaching the night white. Hardik Pandya watches it from the dugout first. Helmet on his knees, gloves half-strapped. India is chasing 294. Comfortable on paper but never comfortable in the middle. He knows this.

Australia had looked in control earlier. Too much control, maybe. Aaron Finch, calm and unbothered, had driven them to 232 for 2 in

40 overs. The scoreboard glared. Aaron's century carried an authority. Then something cracked. The last 10 overs felt rushed, almost panicked. Just 59 runs and four wickets gone. From thoughts of 350 to a modest 293 for 6 – a chance left ajar. Now it's India's turn.

Rohit Sharma and Ajinkya Rahane had walked out first, unhurried and unafraid. Rohit scored seventy-one and Rahane scored seventy. A 131-run opening stand that softened the chase, lowered the pulse. The crowd had found its rhythm – claps instead of gasps. But cricket never lets a story stay simple.

The openers begin to fall. Then Virat Kohli went for 28, searching for timing. Kedar Jadhav – just two, barely settled. The energy shifts – not panic yet, but concern. The asking rate rises, and Australia sense an opportunity. This is the moment they were waiting for.

Then Hardik rises. The walk to the crease feels longer than usual. He adjusts his helmet and tightens the gloves. The sounds fall to

INDIA

the wayside. *Just bat. Just stay.* He reminds himself he's been here before – Chennai, the series opener, pressure sitting heavy on his shoulders then too. First ball, he lets it go. It's outside off stump. A statement in restraint. The next one is shorter. He swivels, pulls – not brutal, just precise. The ball skims the grass and kisses the boundary rope. The crowd exhales. He's in. The innings doesn't explode. It builds. He takes singles when they're there and runs for two when he can. He keeps the scoreboard moving, eyes always flicking to the scores and recalculating. *Don't rush. Don't stall.*

Spin comes on. It's Ashton Agar, and Australia wants control again. Hardik steps out and lifts the ball over mid-on. Not quite six, but safe enough. Then the sweep – powerful, not a pretty four. A floated delivery disappears straight and high. It's a huge Six. The stadium shakes. Four sixes come off Agar in all, each one loosening Australia's grip, each one keeping the rate

INDIA

honest. At the other end, Manish Pandey settles in with quiet confidence. They don't talk much. They don't need to. The partnership grows – 78 runs for the fifth wicket. Calm, professional work. The chase tilts in India's favour.

There are anxious moments still. A misfield, almost caught. A mistimed pull that lands safely. Hardik feels the thin line under his boots with every ball. *Stay balanced. Stay present.* The 50 arrives not with a roar, but with control. He raises the bat briefly. No theatrics, as he knows there's still work left.

Fast bowlers return. Short balls test him. He pulls one flat for six. He ducks the next. When a yorker comes, he squeezes it past the fielders for a four. Every response feels deliberate, like he's answering questions Australia keeps asking too late. Then, finally, the end. Another short ball. He goes for it – muscle memory taking over. This time, the timing slips. The catch is taken. A brief silence, then applause.

AUSTRALIA

Hardik looks once at the pitch. He has scored 78 runs in 72 balls. His job is almost done. No helmet toss and no glare. Just a nod as he walks back. India finishes the chase soon after. It's a five-wicket win with 13 balls to spare. A 3–0 series lead. India reclaims the number one spot. But the night belongs to the stretch in between – the moment when the chase could have wobbled, and didn't. Hardik didn't just finish this game. He held it steady until it stopped shaking.

> *'It feels pretty good but I would like to finish the game next time. I don't need to be surprised. It is important to back myself, and [I] saw it as an opportunity.'*
>
> – HARDIK PANDYA

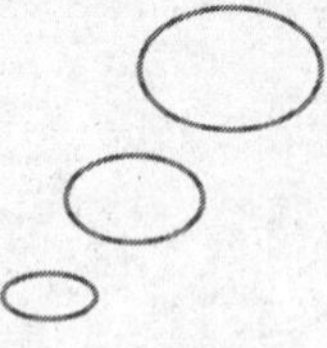

6

HARDIK LEADS THE TITANS TO TRIUMPH

29 MAY 2022, NARENDRA MODI STADIUM, AHMEDABAD

The blue and gold colours ripple through a stadium that feels less like a concrete building and more like a living thing – breathing, waiting, watching. Over 100,000 people. Night pressing down, lights blazing up. It's the 2022 IPL men's final: Gujarat Titans versus Rajasthan Royals.

Captain Hardik Pandya stands still. An all-rounder at the centre of everything. He lost the toss. Same pitch as the qualifier. Dry, used and tricky. His fingers roll the ball once, twice. He knows what this surface will give. And what it will take away. The match begins, and the noise rises high.

When Rajasthan Royals begin their innings, Jos Buttler struggles to find rhythm. He pushes and misses early, scoring slowly at 10 off 14 balls. The crowd murmurs. Hardik hears the impatience and the opportunity. When the edge finally comes, the ball goes straight into the hands of the wicketkeeper. Buttler gone for 39 – it feels inevitable, like gravity doing its job.

Before that, Yashasvi Jaiswal had tried to break free. Eight balls without a run. Then a flash – a full-length delivery by Mohammed Shami and boundaries over extra-cover. Yash Dayal pulls him back into line. Jaiswal falls for 22 off 16 at deep square leg. Silence follows. Sanju Samson walks in fast, as if speed can undo some of the pressure, and hits two early fours. Confidence flickers, but Hardik bangs it in with a hard length. Samson shapes big, too big. The ball flies a backward point where Sai Kishore waits and takes the catch. Hardik doesn't smile.

He stays calm and keeps pounding. Devdutt Padikkal can't move him. Seven balls, zero runs. The bat finally swings – not at Hardik, but at Rashid. Backward point again. Two off 10. Another breath was sucked out of the Royals' dressing room.

Shimron Hetmyer tries to settle but can't. Hardik gives him nothing. Then gives him everything – a return catch, gently looping back, plopping into his own hands – 11 off 12. The spell is complete. Four overs, seventeen runs and three wickets. No fear in the body. No hesitation in the shoulder. Bouncers north of 140. This isn't survival. This is a command.

Rajasthan limped to the end: Ravichandran Ashwin and Trent Boult, one after the other. Sai Kishore is introduced at just the right moment. He delivers overs 16 and 18 like a promise kept. Ashwin and Boult gone. Shami finishes it – Riyan Parag's off stump uprooted on the last ball. Rajasthan Royals are 130 for 9. Everyone's

189
HETTIE
MRF

celebrating, but Hardik walks off knowing it's enough, knowing it isn't safe.

The chase begins badly. Prasidh Krishna through Wriddhiman Saha. Boult with a maiden, squeezing the air out of the innings. Matthew Wade swings once for six then perishes, leaving the Titans wobbling at 23 for 2. Shubman Gill is there – a quiet, anchored presence. A dropped catch on zero gives him life. He doesn't waste it. Hardik pads up slowly. Ties his laces tighter than usual and thinks the same thing all over again. *Stay calm. Stay long.*

He starts slow – 11 off 17. The asking rate whispers and pressure leans in. At halfway, it's 54 for 2. Seventy-seven needed off 10 overs. The stadium hums again – not loud yet, but tense. Then the switch – two fours, a six off Ashwin. A 50-run partnership. The ball suddenly looks smaller. The field looks larger.

Yuzvendra Chahal is called to bowl. The ball lands on the pitch and spins away from Hardik,

who attempts a shot, but the ball hits the outside edge of his bat instead of the middle. The ball flies from the edge to Yashasvi Jaiswal, who catches it. Hardik is gone for 34 off 30. Titans still need 45. The purple cap changes hands, but Hardik's job is already done. He walks back, eyes on the middle, trusting what he's set in motion.

David Miller arrives like an answer and joins Gill. Together, they accelerate the innings efficiently. Twenty-two out of twenty-four becomes easier – 13 in an over. Boundaries flow, the Royals fade and Gill ends it the way he has played it all – clean, high, over the rope. A maximum. Forty-five not out and 11 balls to spare.

Hardik stands near the boundary rope watching the conclusion, feeling the weight of a debut season conclude in a maiden title. A captain who bowled, batted, decided and trusted. Cricket tonight was not a game. It was

HARDIK
33

JAISWAL
23

a performance, and Hardik Pandya was at its centre, long before the last run was scored.

> *'Cricket has taught me the value of hard work and dedication. It's not just a game; it's a way of life.'*
>
> — HARDIK PANDYA

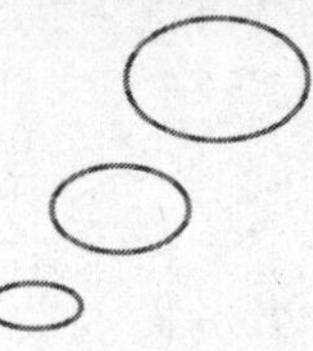

7

THE BRUTAL BOUNCER

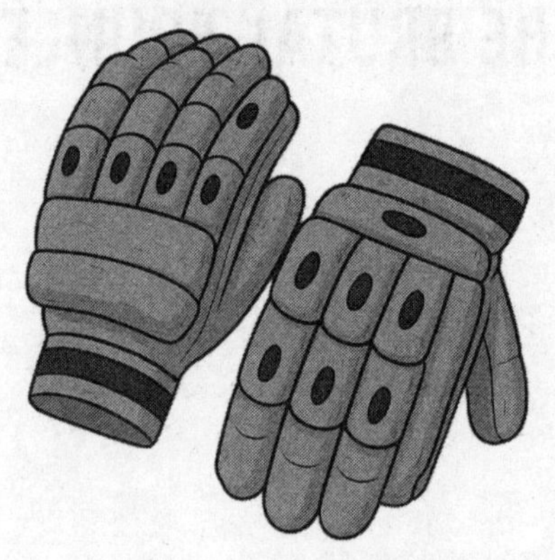

The murmur of expectation swells into something heavier. The sounds of Pune are already a loud, constant thrum, but it sharpens the moment Hardik Pandya begins his run-up. He takes the ball, feels the seam, exhales at the beginning of the ninth over. This is his first of the day.

This is routine. This is control. He runs in – a smooth, familiar motion. The follow-through comes – and then it doesn't. Something twists. Not a crack. Not a pop. Just a sudden jolt that shoots up from the left ankle and steals his balance for half a second too long. His foot lands where it shouldn't. His body knows before his mind does.

Not now. He stops and bends forward with his hands on knees. The crowd's roar becomes muted. He straightens, tests the ankle with a tiny shift of weight. Pain answers immediately, sharp and insistent. The physio is already sprinting out, his blue kit cutting through the green. Fingers probing, pressing, rotating. Hardik stares at the pitch, jaw tight, eyes unfocused. This is the World Cup at home. You don't limp in a World Cup.

He tries to bowl again. Tries to convince the ankle. One step, two – and the message is unmistakable. Too much. Far too much. Barely an hour into the game, and he walks off slowly. Each step is deliberate. The stadium watches in uneasy silence as Virat Kohli takes the ball to finish the over. Three deliveries that feel strangely distant, as they belong to another match entirely. Later, the broadcast confirms it. Hardik Pandya will not return for the rest of the innings. Scans to follow.

INDIA
INDIA
INDIA
INDIA

In the presentation ceremony, Rohit Sharma chooses his words carefully. 'He pulled up a bit sore. There's no major damage. That is good for us.' He takes a pause and then adds with honesty. 'With an injury like that, you've got to assess every day.'

Every day. That phrase lingers. Because Hardik knows what he means to this side, he isn't just another name on the team sheet. He is the balance. The sixth bowler and the all-rounder who lets India breathe easier.

In the first three matches of this World Cup, he had bowled 16 overs and taken five wickets. Rohit had trusted him, sending him in before the specialist fast bowler, Shardul Thakur. India had been careful with his workload precisely because of this moment – because if he goes down, there is no like-for-like replacement.

Shardul can bat at number seven, but then the bowling thins. Bring in another batter, and suddenly, five bowlers must carry 10 overs each.

INDIA

This team is built around Hardik's presence, even when he isn't touching the ball.

India remains unbeaten with three wins from three. But New Zealand is waiting in Dharamsala. Another unbeaten opponent. Another big night looming. And Hardik is walking into the unknown. What the crowd doesn't see is what comes next – the quiet rooms, the swelling, the pain that refuses to fade, the desperation. Hardik pushes harder than he should. Injections – three different places in the ankle. Blood was drawn to reduce the swelling. The logic is brutal: if there is even a 1 per cent chance, he will take it.

'I didn't want to give up,' he says later. 'For the team, I will give my best.'

He knows the risk. He knows what forcing a body can do. But this is a home World Cup. This is not negotiable. While he pushes himself, the injury returns. Then deepens. What could have been managed becomes something else

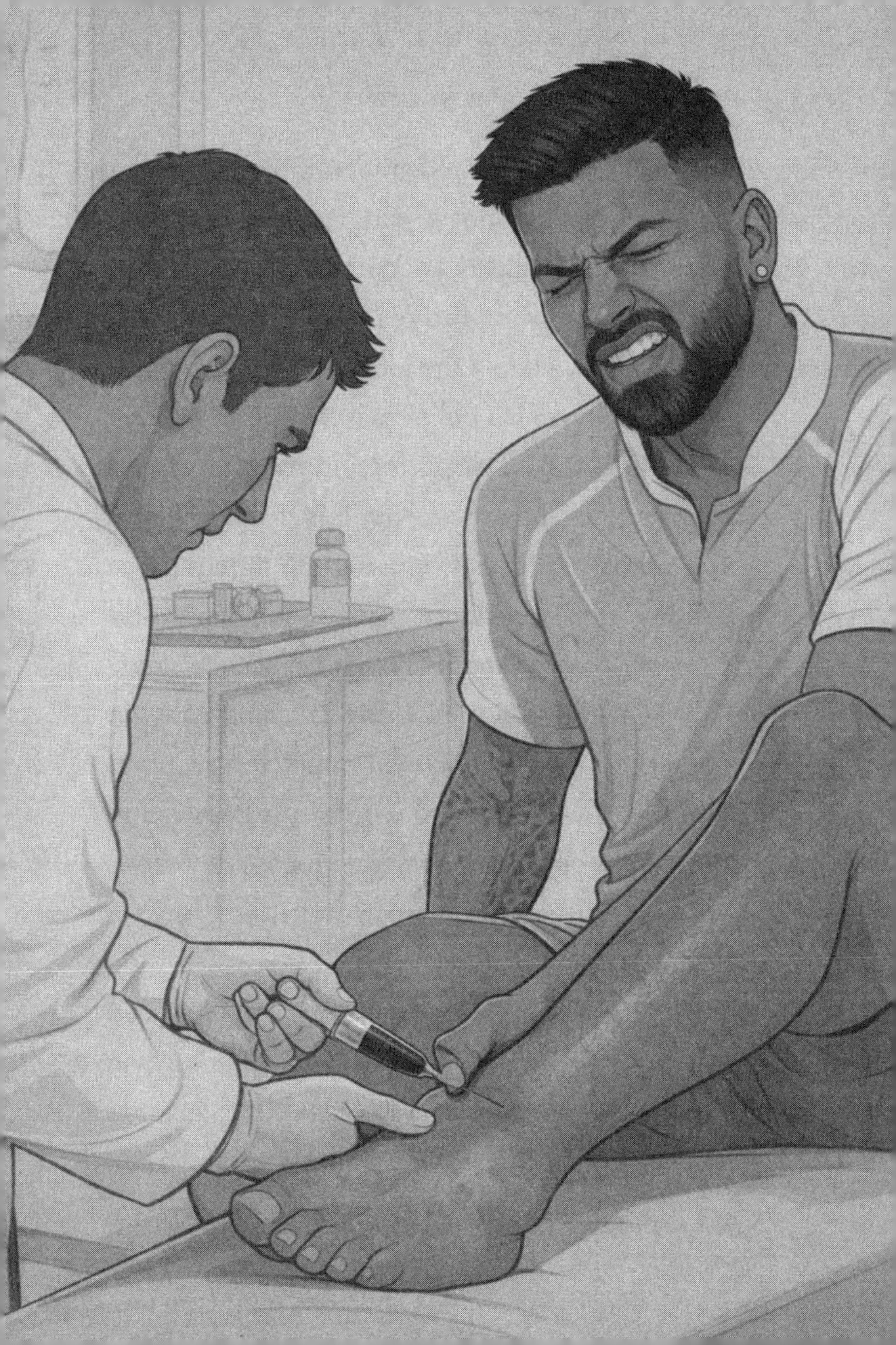

entirely. A three-month injury. Days when he cannot walk, yet tries to run. Painkillers dull the signals, but his body keeps screaming.

When he first leaves the field against Bangladesh, he tells the team he will be back in five days. *Five.* He believes it. Needs to believe it. He tries for 10 days, forcing movement and ignoring consequences. But it is a freak injury. The rehab stretches from what he thought was 25 days into something much longer. The World Cup moves on without him. That absence stays.

'For me, the biggest pride is to play for the country,' he admits. 'Playing the World Cup at home is my child.' The words are heavy and personal. Missing the momentous event does not fade. It waits, presses, and it will always be there.

This wasn't a rushed preparation. He had started a year earlier. Planned routines one and a half years in advance. He had calculated every step, and every session was intentional.

And still, one misstep in a follow-through changes everything.

Cricket does that. In a game measured by numbers – overs bowled, wickets taken, wins stacked neatly in columns – it still turns on moments you can't quantify. A twisted ankle. A walk-off at 2.59 p.m. A silence where noise should be.

Hardik Pandya's World Cup ends not with a final ball, but with the slow, painful understanding that sometimes the hardest battles happen before you ever get the chance to act.

'For me, I've always been very fortunate to play for the country. It was a freak injury which happened [in the 2023 World Cup]. I tried to come back, but God had some other plans. The other day, I was speaking to Rahul Sir, and he said luck comes to people who work hard. That has stuck with me, and I just want to keep my head down and keep working hard.'

— HARDIK PANDYA

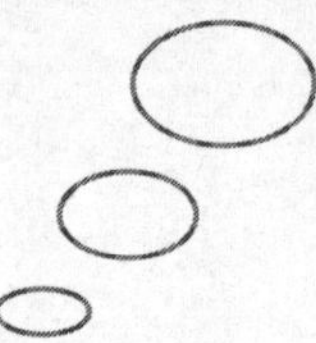

8

THE LUNCH CAN WAIT

13 AUGUST 2017, PALLEKELE, SRI LANKA

The atmosphere in Pallekele is already abuzz: the morning heat humming, fielders clapping and layers of noise. A murmur that never fully dies. India is 329 for 6. The innings feels fragile, like glass left on the edge of a table.

Hardik Pandya stands at the non-striker's end, chewing the inside of his cheek. *We bat time first. Noise later.* Wriddhiman is with him, careful and watchful. They're trying to rebuild, not explode. But the day's ninth ball has other plans. Vishwa Fernando bowls a bouncer. Wriddhiman tries to play the ball but only manages to hit it with the edge of his bat. Standing in the gully was Dilruwan Perera, who takes the catch, and Saha is gone for 16 runs. India is now 339 for 7. The sound spikes, then settles into that sharp, hungry silence bowlers love. Pandya looks away toward square leg. *So much for quiet.*

Kuldeep Yadav walks in, thin shoulders, stubborn eyes. The runs don't come easy. Fernando beats him – outside edge, inside edge, leg before wicket shout. Four times in a spell. The pitch is talking now. The bowlers circle. Pandya answers in singles, in patience, in respect. Short ball – pulled. Width – punched. Nothing wild. Not yet. Together, they add 62 runs for the eighth wicket. India crawls past 400 in the one-hundred and tenth over. It had seemed distant at stumps on day one. Now it's real. Then Lakshan Sandakan dips one, finds Kuldeep's edge. At 26 runs off 73 balls, Kuldeep is gone.

Pandya watches him leave. *Time's up.*

KULDEEP
23

INDIA

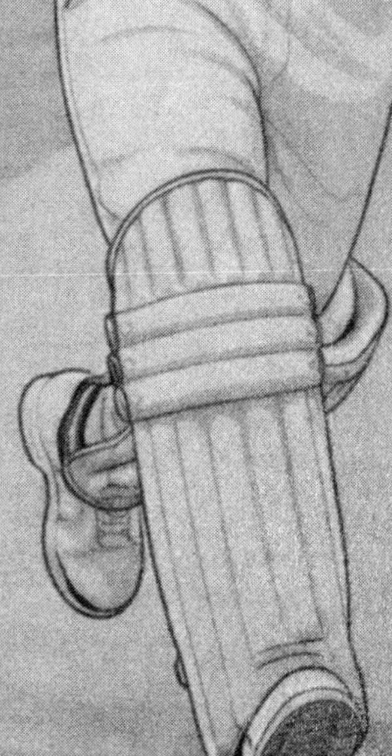

Mohammed Shami arrives. The field creeps in. Malinda Pushpakumara begins his one hundred and sixteenth over. Pandya is at the striker's end. First ball – Hardik plays a slog sweep, sending the ball for a four. He lofts the second ball, sending it flat past the bowler. Then three straight sixes with still head and full swing. Twenty-six runs in the over. Sight-screen rattles. History shifts – it is the most runs by an Indian in a Test over, surpassing the old 24 by Kapil Dev and Sandeep Patil. The crowd is no longer a crowd. It's the weather.

Pandya reaches his half-century off 61 balls somewhere in the blur. Shami adds eight before Sandakan takes a return catch. But momentum has already changed shape. Umesh Yadav comes in. Bat raised like a grin. Pandya doesn't look at him. *Stay with me,* he thinks to himself. They explode – a 50-run stand-off, 26 balls for the last wicket. Lunch is delayed. Bowlers try wide lines, short deliveries, and slower balls.

INDIA

It doesn't matter. Pandya hooks, drives, and whips the ball with fearless authority. Umesh contributes three runs, and Pandya makes most of the noise.

In the middle of it, almost casually, Pandya reaches three figures. His second 50 comes in just 25 balls. He is 108 not out at lunch off 93 balls, of which he has hit eight fours and seven sixes. Hardik becomes the first Indian to score a Test hundred before lunch. This is his highest first-class score, the second fastest for an Indian player overseas after Virender Sehwag's 78-ball hundred in 2006. He removes his helmet. Breath fogs the grill. *Don't wake up.* India is 487. But the day isn't done with him. Sri Lanka begins brightly, then Shami dismantles the top order with upright seam and perfect length, dismissing Dimuth Karunaratne and Upul Tharanga as edges fly and feet remain frozen. Pressure builds steadily. Kuldeep settles, later ripping through with 4 for 40. Pandya, first change now, pins

S
S
INDIA

Angelo Mathews leg before wicket with a low one. Sri Lanka is folded for 135 in 37.4 overs. Follow-on is enforced. By stumps, they are 19 for 1, trailing by 333 runs. Yet the image that lingers isn't a wicket. It's from earlier. Pushpakumara is running in. Pandya is still, his bat raised. The moment stretches. *They know I can hit. I know they know. Now we stop pretending*. Cricket, for a while, stops being a game. It becomes a confrontation. Breath against breath. Nerve against nerve. And Hardik Pandya, in that rising storm, stands exactly where the story turns.

> *'I believe in the process, and I believe in working hard every day to improve.'*
>
> — HARDIK PANDYA

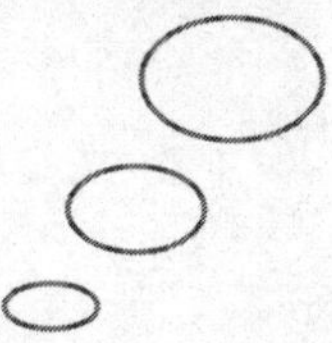

9

THE FIERY FINISH

4 MARCH 2025, DUBAI, INDIA VERSUS AUSTRALIA, CHAMPIONS TROPHY 2025

The stadium does not erupt; it tightens. Conversations taper into expectation, and thousands of small movements – hands adjusting caps, cameras lifting, shoulders leaning forward – fall into rhythm. The scoreboard glows with possibility rather than certainty. India versus Australia again, but the memory of 2023 still hangs around like unfinished business. Hardik Pandya sits unusually still. He doesn't look at the giant screen. He doesn't need to.

Finals have long memories, his mind whispers. *So do I.*

Australia bats first. Travis Head comes out swinging – 39 off 33 – strokes flashing like camera bulbs before Varun Chakravarthy finds the edge and Gill holds on. The dismissal brings a sharp roar from the crowd.

Cooper Connolly scratches, stalls, nine balls of hesitation, then KL Rahul takes the catch off Shami in the third over. Silence from one half of the ground. Excitement from the other. Marnus Labuschagne grinds out 29 runs from 36 balls, and Inglis makes 11 runs. The innings breathe but never relax. Then Alex Carey walks in. Steve Smith is already there, calm, deliberate, captain-like. They tighten the threads as they make a 50-run partnership.

Smith reaches 73. Then Shami happens. He bowls straight into the wickets, and the off stump leans back. Glenn Maxwell follows for seven, Axar knocking him over. Suddenly, the

CONNOLLY
9
RAHUL
1

Australian middle order feels fragile. But Carey keeps pushing with quick feet and fast hands. He races to 61 before a run-out in the forty-eighth over. Adam Zampa and Nathan Ellis are also gone in the last two overs. Australia is all out for 264, the highest total in Dubai in this tournament, with three balls remaining. A score that sits heavily.

Hardik watches from the boundary rope, palms at the back. *264. Not impossible. Not easy. Perfect.*

India begins chasing. Ben Dwarshuis bowls Gill. Rohit is trapped leg before wicket by Connolly. India is 43 for 2 after eight overs. The sound inside the stadium changes pitch – sharper, nervous, metallic. Shreyas Iyer finds rhythm and draws out 45 runs before Zampa crashes through his stumps. Kohli stands at one end, while Axar joins at the other. The chase becomes calculation, not emotion. When Ellis bowls Axar, KL Rahul walks in. The game tightens its grip.

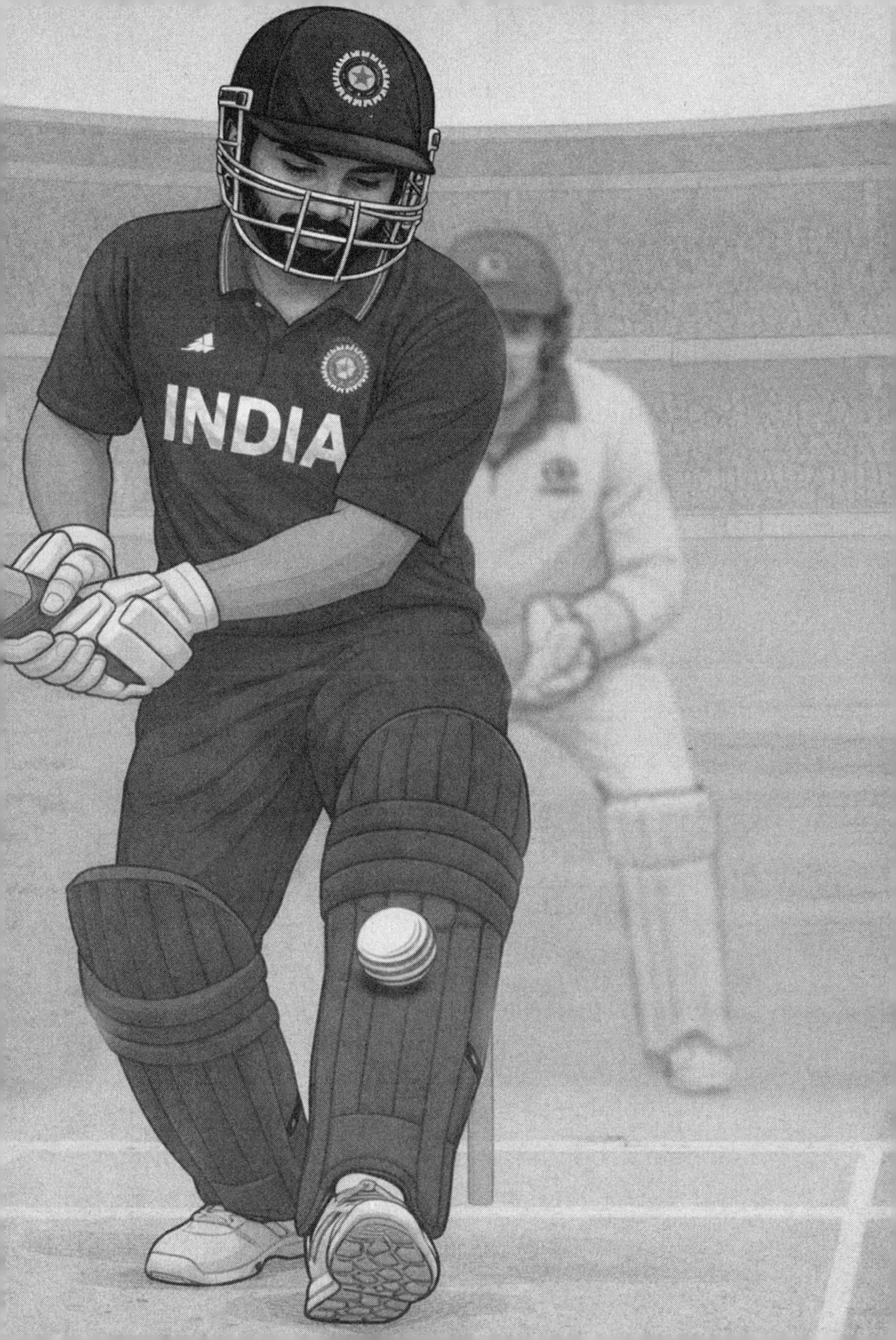
INDIA

Kohli builds his innings patiently, breath by breath and shot by shot. He makes 84 runs – an innings of control in a room full of chaos. But even that doesn't conclude the story. Kohli misreads the ball outside off early but still trusts himself to hit it over long-on. The strike lacks full power, the ball hangs in the night, and Dwarshuis completes the catch.

Now, the slow motion begins. The scoreboard reads 225/5. India needs 40 from 44 balls to win. Hardik Pandya stands at the top of the steps. His spikes scrape the concrete. One lace loose. He bends to tighten it. He inhales deeply and exhales slowly. *They think this is pressure,* he smiles inwardly. *This is space.*

In the dressing room, the mood is tense. Axar will later joke about it – *just singles, just twos!* – half a prayer, half an instruction. But Hardik senses something different. He's laughing inside. He can feel the moment bending. First swing: clean. Then the

INDIA

one that changes everything – Zampa over the wicket. Hardik clears his front leg and launches a massive six. The ball disappears into colour and noise. Then comes the back-to-back sixes. Momentum doesn't shift; it flips.

Rahul holds one end, precise, controlled. Hardik is the thunder. He races to 28 runs off 24 balls, three sixes and a boundary, each strike louder than the last. The field spreads. The Australians talk faster. Movements get sharper, less certain. *This is my time,* he thinks, almost amused. *Why rush fear? Let it come to me.*

In the forty-ninth over, Hardik falls. A catch in the deep. He walks off, having given the team 28 runs off 24 balls. There are no showy displays. Just a nod. He knows that he has altered the balance of the match. Now, the match is in favour of India. Rahul remains at 42 off 34. Jadeja faces one ball, scores two – a tiny brush stroke in a vibrant painting. Then Rahul finishes it with a six. India is 267/6. It's a four-wicket win.

INDIA

The roar returns all at once. But Hardik doesn't look up immediately. He looks at his gloves. Flexes his fingers. *Laughing inside,* he reminds himself. Because before the shot, before the sixes, before the scorecard – there was only a man at the top of the stairs, tying his laces, while the world shook.

'Whatever I have learned in my career so far in nine or ten years, if I am able to share my experiences with newer guys, I am not helping just him, but just helping my team. If I am able to contribute even one per cent and that player is able to perform better, that has always been my mindset.'

– HARDIK PANDYA

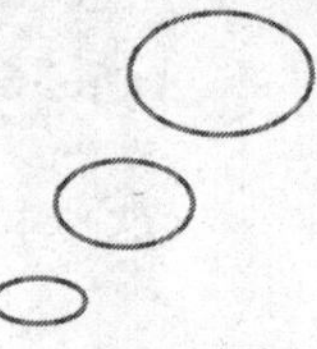

10

VELOCITY

19 DECEMBER 2025, NARENDRA MODI STADIUM, AHMEDABAD

The lights feel too bright tonight, white and harsh, buzzing like insects over hot concrete. The stadium in Ahmedabad trembles with a steady din, memory, expectation – the same ground that once roared *against* him now hums with something uncertain, almost curious.

South Africa had come to India and taken two famous Tests. That sting still lingers in memory, an unfinished resolution. But this is the fifth and final T20I. A Friday night that serves as the last word of the tour. India wants it badly. They are put in to bat. The Powerplay is a blur of elevation and intent – Sanju Samson is playing at 37 runs in 22 balls, carving angles with four fours and two sixes, and Abhishek Sharma is with him at 34 runs off 21 balls, riding bounce with six fours and a six. The ball is a white streak under floodlights. The sound is constant as the bat meets the ball, the crowd roars, and the rhythm repeats without a pause.

Then three is a stutter, a pause in the rhythm. Suryakumar Yadav is out at five runs off seven balls. A scratchy stay and a quiet exit. The noise dips, uneasy, like a crowd clearing its throat.

Not now. Keep it moving. Hardik walks in at five. Slow steps, heavy breathing and gloves pressed together. The crease looks small, but the boundary ropes seem closer than usual. He doesn't look at the crowd. Not yet. He closes his eyes and recalls the 2024 T20 international against South Africa.

INDIA
SG

The memory came crashing – Barbados, the humid night clinging to the skin, 176 in 20 overs already on the board, yet feeling breakable. He had felt that same dryness in his mouth when the board read 26 needed off 24, Klaasen swinging like a storm. *Breathe. One ball decides nothing. One spell can.* The crowd had been boisterous, but inside there was only the thud of his pulse and the seam against his fingers, as he walked back to his mark, knowing moments like these did not ask for heroes – they exposed them. Klaasen reached, a faint edge, straight into the keeper's gloves – Klaasen dismissed. What followed felt physical, a wave hitting bone. He turned, breathing hard, reminding himself the storm still had a name: Miller. Six balls and sixteen runs to defend. *One over. Stay here.*

He returned for the last over and felt the wind tug towards the dressing room, a secret he half-trusted, half-feared. He bowled a full toss. Miller swung his bat. The ball climbed, hung,

RDIK
3
INDIA
SOUTH
AFRICA

and the world narrowed to white against black sky. Suryakumar ran left from long-off, took the catch, flicked it up as momentum carried him over the rope, stepped back in and completed the catch. Then the wait – the third umpire check, hearts suspended – until OUT flashing at last on the big screen. A drop from Rishabh Pant, a boundary, 12 off 4; singles, 10 off 2; a wide, 9 off 2. Then Rabada fell, his third wicket, again to Suryakumar. South Africa 168/8 in 19.5. A single to end: 169/8. India had won by seven runs. Seventeen years released in a breath he didn't know he was holding, and he stood still under the Barbados sky, shoulders lightening, a smile arriving slowly as India became the champions again.

He opens his eyes with confidence. *First ball. Commit.*

The bowler runs in with the seam upright and delivers a ball that is neither full nor short enough, Hardik Pandya steps out and swings

HARDIK
33

his bat with power. The ball climbs into the night – clean, arrogant, absolute. It's a six on the very first ball. He doesn't smile. Just nods to himself. *Told you.* Order returns and aggression reasserts itself.

Tilak Varma at the other end has already made 73 runs off 42 balls, with 10 fours and one six, mirroring the tempo, and together they don't build a partnership; they *detonate* one. One hundred and five runs off 44 balls added for the fourth wicket. Boundaries smear across the outfield. Fielders run patterns that lead nowhere. Hardik's bat feels lighter with every swing. Length balls disappear, width is punished and pace is borrowed only to be redirected. The innings becomes a series of early decisions, struck earlier.

He races to 63 off 25 balls, five fours, five sixes – a late surge that bends the match. By the time he holes out in the last over, India are well past 200, finishing 231 for 5. And then he

HARDIK
33

hears it. Thundering applause. The whole stadium rises. The venue that once greeted him with hostility after the IPL switch now stands as one. The noise washes over him, not loud, but deep. *Funny game.*

South Africa chases 232 with belief. Quinton de Kock scores 65 off 35 balls with clean hitting and free arms. The visitors match India's tempo, glide through the Powerplay, and suddenly it's 118 for 1 at the halfway mark, making the contest balanced and dangerous. Dewald Brevis joins the flow. The pressure swings. *This is slipping.* Suryakumar Yadav turns, takes one look and calls upon Bumrah. He runs in with the calm of someone who knows timing is everything – a slower ball. De Kock checks the shot too late, resulting in a return catch that is safely taken. The sound changes again and grows sharper, as hope edged with disbelief.

Next over, Hardik tries something different – a slower bouncer. Brevis is hurried. Another

INDIA
INDIA

breakthrough. Then Varun Chakravarthy takes control in the decisive thirteenth over. Aiden Markram is trapped on the pads, and Ferreira is bowled. The chase fractures and the control collapses within a few minutes.

In three overs, South Africa crashed from 120 for 1 to 135 for 5. Bumrah returns for a miserly seventeenth over – just two runs. The door doesn't just close, it locks. Varun finishes with 4/53, Bumrah with 2/17 and Hardik chips in with one wicket. South Africa ended on 201/8. India wins by 30 runs, and the Series is sealed 3–1 at the Narendra Modi Stadium. Ten consecutive series wins now. The streak grows. Later, in the quiet after the storm, Hardik shrugs when told he struck the second-fastest 50 for India.

'I missed the top spot?' A half-smile. 'I told my partner I'd step out first ball and hit six. The situation suited my style. I took a calculated risk. It worked.' He says setbacks don't matter.

INDIA

You come back stronger and the work never stops – that matters.

But tonight, something came full circle. Cricket, for those loud, breathless hours, wasn't a game. It was a theatre. And Hardik Pandya, 'player of the match', owned the stage.

INDIA

'My focus is not on stats; it's all about how I can win games for my country.'

— HARDIK PANDYA

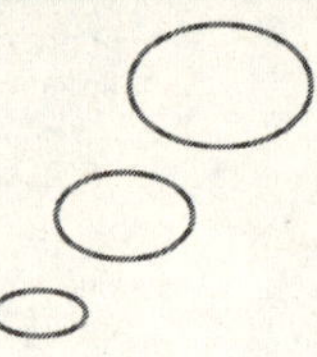

11

HARDIK PANDYA: THE MAN

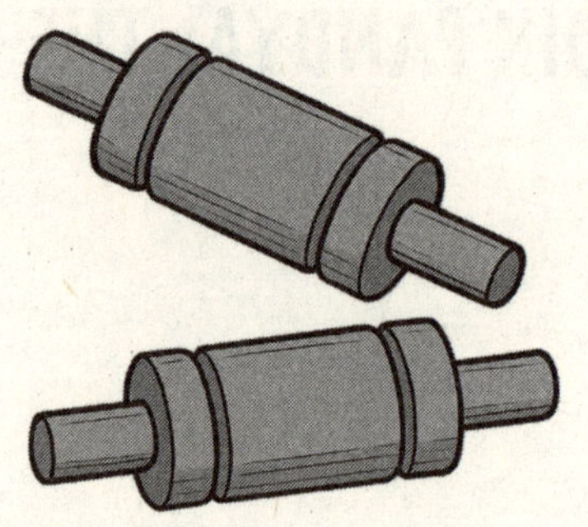

Hardik Pandya lives with his brother, Krunal, his sister-in-law, Pankhuri, and his son, Agastya, in a luxurious apartment in Mumbai. He owns a penthouse in Vadodara, Gujarat, where he frequently lives with his family.

Hardik tied the knot with Serbian model, actress and dancer, Nataša Stankovic, and shortly after, the couple welcomed their son, Agastya Pandya. After four years together, they separated amicably and continue to co-parent their son lovingly.

Away from cricket, Hardik has a range of hobbies and interests that offer a glimpse into his personality beyond being a sportsperson. He

enjoys travelling, listening to music – especially Punjabi and R&B – and spending quality time with friends and family. He is a fitness enthusiast who regularly shares parts of his workout routine on social media and maintains rigorous training to balance his demanding schedule.

Hardik is known for his stylish looks, bold haircuts and a love of tattoos. He owns an impressive collection of luxury cars, including a Mercedes G-Wagon, an Audi A6, a Jeep Compass and a Lamborghini Huracan. He is frequently seen wearing high-end watches.

Hardik is nicknamed 'Kung Fu Pandya' in the cricketing world because of his energetic, impactful playing style. Outside sporting commitments, Hardik has been involved in generous social causes, notably contributing during the Covid-19 pandemic with financial and medical assistance alongside his brother.

When he's off duty, Hardik enjoys watching films and enjoys the work of Akshay Kumar and

Alia Bhatt. He is also a football fan, following teams like Manchester United. He has a fondness for Gujarati cuisine, which connects him to his roots and family culture.

'I live for the moment. I'm not thinking too far ahead, I'm just enjoying the journey.'

— HARDIK PANDYA

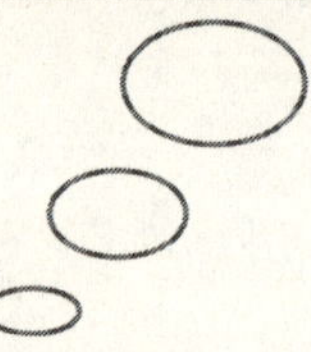

12

EPILOGUE

PLUS
2000

When Hardik Himanshu Pandya first walked onto a dusty local ground in Gujarat, his dream was simple – play good cricket and make his family proud while chasing a dream that seemed far away. Over the years, that dream took shape in magnificent ways. Early in his cricketing days, Hardik began as a leg-spin bowler before being encouraged to try medium-pace, a pivot that defined his future as a fast-bowling all-rounder. Hardik's arrival in international cricket in 2016 marked the beginning of a new force in Indian cricket as a fierce all-rounder who could change the course of a match with both bat and ball. From scoring crucial runs to delivering vital overs, his impact has been undeniable. As of 2026, he continues to represent India in all formats and even marked a decade in international cricket with a heartfelt tribute, saying he's 'only just getting started'.

His IPL journey has been equally remarkable. After rising to prominence with the Mumbai Indians, Hardik captained the Gujarat Titans to their first title in their debut season – a unique feat in franchise history. In later years, he returned to the Mumbai League and briefly led the Indians, navigating praise and criticism as he sought to solidify his legacy as a leader.

Hardik's story is not just about his cricketing talent; it's the continuing evolution of the man behind the performance. From battling early financial struggles to achieving success on the international stage, Hardik's journey embodies resilience. At 32, he remains a central figure in India's cricketing plans, inspiring young players with both his performance and his refusal to be defined by setbacks.

This is his era of growth, not a conclusion, but an epilogue that hints at more chapters yet to be written. As Hardik himself has acknowledged, even with a decade behind him, his *true story is still unfolding*.

'I believe in grace. A lot was said by people who don't even know me one percent as a person... I have always believed in life that you never respond with words, circumstances can respond.'

— HARDIK PANDYA

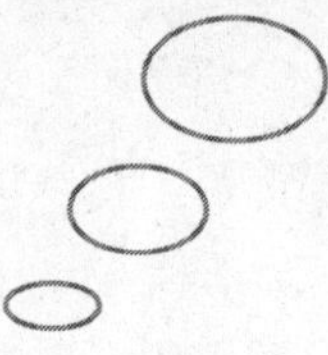

HARDIK PANDYA: THE FACT FILE

Hardik made his India debut in January 2016 and has since evolved into a senior all-rounder, combining power-hitting, useful medium-fast bowling and athletic fielding. He is known for being a match-finisher with the bat and a key death overs bowler. Despite injuries and workload management challenges, he remains central to India's white-ball squads. He holds unique statistical milestones in T20 cricket, has multiple IPL titles (including as captain), and has been pivotal in India's recent ICC trophy triumphs.

- **Batting Style:** Right-handed batsman
- **Bowling Style:** Right-arm medium-fast
- **Role:** All-rounder (batting all-rounder/ finisher)

DOMESTIC (FIRST-CLASS AND LIST-A)

First-Class: 29 matches, 1351 runs (HS 108), 48 wickets (best 8/91).

MAJOR ACHIEVEMENTS AND MILESTONES

International Achievements

- First Indian to achieve both 100 wickets and 1000+ runs in T20 Internationals.
- Second-fastest Indian to score a T20I 50 (16-ball 50 versus South Africa).
- Became one of the few Indian batters with 100+ sixes in T20Is.
- Long-standing all-round contributor for India across Tests, ODIs and T20Is.
- Notable match-winning performances and clutch innings in key bilateral games and ICC events.

ICC and Tournament Success

- Played major roles in India's ICC T20 World Cup victory (2024).
- Key contributor in India's ICC Champions Trophy win (2025).

IPL and Franchise Highlights

- Five-time IPL winner:
  – Four titles with the Mumbai Indians (as a player: 2015, 2017, 2019, 2020)
  – One title with the Gujarat Titans (as captain: 2022)
- Captaincy: Excellent leadership with the Gujarat Titans (win percentage: ~57 per cent).

FEATS

FIRST INDIAN TO ACHIEVE BOTH 100 WICKETS AND 1000+ RUNS IN T20 INTERNATIONALS

SECOND-FASTEST INDIAN TO A HALF-CENTURY - T20I

FIVE-TIME IPL WINNER

TEST FORMAT

BOWLING

Stat	Value
MATCHES	11
STRIKE RATE	55.12
INNINGS	19
4W	0
BALLS	937
5W	1
RUNS	528
10W	0
WICKETS	17
BBI	5/28
AVERAGE	31.06
BBM	6/50
ECONOMY RATE	3.38

TEST FORMAT

BATTING / FIELDING

11 MATCHES	73.89 STRIKE RATE
18 INNINGS	1 CENTURIES
1 NOT OUTS	4 HALF-CENTURIES
532 RUNS	12 SIXES
108 HIGHEST SCORE	684 FOURS
31.29 AVERAGE SCORE	7 CATCHES

ODI FORMAT

BOWLING

Stat	Value
MATCHES	94
STRIKE RATE	38.02
INNINGS	88
4W	1
BALLS	3460
5W	0
RUNS	3231
10W	0
WICKETS	91
BBI	4/24
AVERAGE	35.51
BBM	4/24
ECONOMY RATE	5.60

ODI FORMAT

BATTING / FIELDING

94

MATCHES

110.89

STRIKE RATE

68

INNINGS

0

CENTURIES

10

NOT OUTS

11

HALF-CENTURIES

1904

RUNS

76

SIXES

92*

HIGHEST SCORE

141

FOURS

32.83

AVERAGE SCORE

35

CATCHES

T20I FORMAT

BOWLING

Stat	Value
MATCHES	134
STRIKE RATE	19.41
INNINGS	121
4W	3
BALLS	2135
5W	0
RUNS	2958
10W	0
WICKETS	110
BBI	4/16
AVERAGE	26.89
BBM	4/16
ECONOMY RATE	8.31

T20I FORMAT

BATTING / FIELDING

134	144.49
MATCHES	STRIKE RATE
105	0
INNINGS	CENTURIES
27	8
NOT OUTS	HALF-CENTURIES
2176	119
RUNS	SIXES
71*	160
HIGHEST SCORE	FOURS
27.90	64
AVERAGE SCORE	CATCHES

IPL FORMAT

BOWLING

Stat	Value
MATCHES	152
STRIKE RATE	20.8
INNINGS	107
4W	1
BALLS	1628
5W	1
RUNS	2492
10W	0
WICKETS	78
BBI	5/36
AVERAGE	31.95
BBM	5/36
ECONOMY RATE	9.18

IPL FORMAT

BATTING / FIELDING

152
MATCHES

146.93
STRIKE RATE

140
INNINGS

0
CENTURIES

43
NOT OUTS

10
HALF-CENTURIES

2749
RUNS

148
SIXES

91
HIGHEST SCORE

207
FOURS

28.34
AVERAGE SCORE

72
CATCHES

FIRST-CLASS

BATTING / FIELDING

MATCHES

STRIKE RATE

INNINGS

1

CENTURIES

NOT OUTS

10

HALF-CENTURIES

1351

RUNS

24

SIXES

108

HIGHEST SCORE

167*

FOURS

30.02

AVERAGE SCORE

14

CATCHES

FIRST-CLASS

BOWLING

Stat	Value
MATCHES	29
STRIKE RATE	56.1
INNINGS	39
4W	0
BALLS	2694
5W	3
RUNS	1486
10W	0
WICKETS	48
BBI	5/28
AVERAGE	30.95
BBM	8/91
ECONOMY RATE	3.30

OTHER BOOKS IN THE SERIES

Surya was all about instincts, but things changed when he learned the rules of cricket to know when and how to break them. From dusty Mumbai gullies to roaring World Cup finals, Surya's journey is packed with daring shots, big comebacks and unforgettable moments, including a gravity-defying catch. In this action-packed, high-energy book, relive the story of a street-smart kid who would one day hold the no. 1 ranking in ICC Men's T20I for an extended period. Here's a warning: once you start reading this book, you may just not be able to stop.

Ravichandran Ashwin has always played the long game. A cricket-mad boy on the streets of Chennai to becoming one of India's greatest match-winners, Ashwin played through illness, injury, doubt and long spells on the sidelines. This book traces his early days at Chepauk, the family that held him steady, the reinventions that shaped his career and the centuries that made him a modern great. From childhood dreams to record-breaking feats, this is the story of a man who never stopped staying in the game. Here's a warning: once you start reading this book, you may just not be able to stop.

You need unshakeable belief to be a champion, no matter where you come from. From growing up as a poor kid whose family couldn't afford his coaching to smashing world records, Rohit's journey has been full of never-give-up moments. Follow him through his school days, his ups and downs, the epic captaincy wins and, of course, the super-duper, totally amazing World Cup. Here's a warning: once you start reading this book, you may just not be able to stop.

Virat Kohli was obsessed with being no. 1 right from the start. So laser-sharp was his focus that he continued to play cricket even after learning that his dad had died – he was only eighteen! In this action-packed, high-energy book, relive his greatest matches, his record-breaking plays and get inside the mind of a champ who turned challenges into victories, lifted cups and inspired millions. Here's a warning: once you start reading this book, you may just not be able to stop.

Once upon a cricket field, there was a boy named Shubman who loved nothing more than hitting the ball out of the park. In 2018, he helped India win the U19 World Cup and was crowned the best player of the tournament. Just a few years later, he would smash a record-breaking double century in ODIs – becoming the youngest Indian to do so. Now 25, and India's Test and ODI captain, he leads the team he once only dreamed of being a part of. Here's a warning: once you start reading this book, you may just not be able to stop.